ALIYA

Volume five of Disney Princess Classic Library

Printed in China

First Edition
1 3 5 7 9 10 8 6 4 2

T425-2382-5-12286
ISBN 978-1-4231-7945-0

For more Disney Press fun, visit www.disneybooks.com
This book was printed on paper created from a sustainable source.

Rapunzel's Heroes

Disney PRESS

New York

THE DAY STARTED NICELY ENOUGH. It was the morning of my eighteenth birthday, and the birds were singing. Just yesterday I'd taken a huge step—I had ventured out from the tall tower that had been my home all my life! And soon, if all went well, I'd be at the kingdom for the first time, watching the beautiful floating lights that were released there every year on the same date . . . my birthday.

It should have been a wonderful morning. But instead, here I was—me, Rapunzel—trying to rescue my guide from a horse!

I wasn't surprised that my guide had a problem with a palace horse. I'd only known Flynn a short while, but he had problems with almost everyone!

So, after I yanked Flynn free, I stepped in front of the horse and stroked his nose. The name on his chest plate was MAXIMUS.

Maximus thought Flynn was a thief (and all right, Flynn was a little misguided). Still, I hoped the horse wouldn't turn him over to the guards—at least, not until I could see the lights. "Today is kind of the biggest day of my life," I explained. "It's also my birthday, just so you know."

Finally, Maximus stuck out his hoof . . . and Flynn shook it.

Together, we set off for the kingdom.
Flynn thought we might travel faster if we rode
on Maximus's back . . . but for some reason,
Maximus did not agree.

Flynn tried again. He even managed to stay on
top of Maximus's head for a few seconds. Then Maximus
lowered his head and Flynn tumbled into the mud again.

"I don't like this horse!" Flynn howled. "And this horse
doesn't like *me*!"

Finally, Flynn decided we'd travel faster if we just started walking.

"Do you have this problem with all horses?" I asked.

"No," Flynn replied. "When I was growing up in the orphanage, I dreamed of becoming a swashbuckling hero—and swashbuckling heroes love horses. No, it's *this* horse. *He's* the problem!"

As we walked, Maximus flicked his tail in Flynn's face. So
Flynn poked Maximus in the ribs. Then Maximus stepped on
Flynn's foot . . . and Flynn yanked on Maximus's bridle.

I sighed. Those two just *had* to get along, or my special day
would be ruined.

Luckily, I had an idea. "I know!" I told Flynn. "I'll *teach* you how
to get along with Maximus!"

Flynn grumbled, but he watched as I stroked Maximus under
the chin. Then I scratched his ears. Pascal, who was sitting on
Maximus's head, helped.

"See?" I said, nuzzling Maximus's face. "Now you do it."

"*Ugh!* No way!" Flynn protested. "That's just plain—"

"NOW!" I commanded.

I don't think I was *too* hard on them.

Getting into the kingdom was a little tricky, because Flynn was wanted by the palace guards. Maximus and Flynn managed it, though, by working together.

Those two were making good progress!

I think Maximus was a little surprised as he watched Flynn that day.

Maybe he realized Flynn wasn't so bad after all. . . .

Maximus still wouldn't let
Flynn climb onto his back,
though.

That evening, when it
was time to see the lanterns
being released, Flynn surprised
me by taking me out in a boat. He
said that watching from the water
would give us the best view.

There was another surprise, too. Flynn
gave Maximus a bag of apples! The horse
looked suspicious.

"What? I bought them," Flynn said.

Maximus whinnied happily as Flynn paddled
away. "Most of them."

We didn't expect to be gone long. Maximus waited and waited.

Finally, a boat bumped up against the dock. But it was a different boat, and it was carrying only Flynn, who was tied to the mast with a stolen crown on his lap! He seemed confused and was yelling, "Rapunzel? Rapunzel!"

Maximus backed out of sight as the palace guards came forward and arrested Flynn. Maximus didn't know where I was, but he knew that something had gone very, very wrong.

Maximus raced away, but he wasn't leaving Flynn. He was going for help!

With a lot of hoof stomping and loud snorting, Maximus convinced our friends at the Snuggly Duckling tavern to follow him back to the castle.

Waving their clubs and axes, they raced for the kingdom, broke into the prison, and freed Flynn.

Of course, getting him *out* of the prison was another problem . . .

. . . but Maximus was ready and waiting!

Together, Max and Flynn galloped through the streets, leaped over guards, and dashed through the town gates just as they were closing.

Flynn could hardly believe he was riding Max. Suddenly, he realized he trusted the horse. They were a team.

I won't explain everything that happened that day, but my life did change forever. Mother Gothel, who had imprisoned me, showed her evil side. Then I learned my true identity. I was a princess and had been stolen from my parents long ago!

But Flynn fought for me. To save me, he had to cut my long golden hair, which magically turned brown. But that didn't matter to me—*or* to him. He loved me for myself.

It was quite a day.

Afterward, we could have ridden back to the kingdom, but Flynn wouldn't allow it. Instead, we *walked!*

"He ran all night," Flynn explained as he patted Maximus. "He's tired and needs a rest." Flynn paused. "You know, I felt like a real hero today." Then he turned to Max. "But you are an even bigger hero. If it weren't for you, Rapunzel and I wouldn't be here."

Flynn and Max were both heroes. But just as important, they were friends.